Maniac Monkeys on Magnolia Street

Maniac Monkeys on Magnolia Street

Angela Johnson
illustrated by John Ward

ALFRED A. KNOPF NEW YORK

THIS IS A BORZOI BOOK PUBLISHED BY ALFRED A. KNOPF, INC.

Published in the United States of America by Alfred A. Knopf, Inc., New York,
and simultaneously in Canada by Random House of Canada Limited, Toronto.
Distributed by Random House, Inc., New York.

www.randomhouse.com/kids

Library of Congress Cataloging-in-Publication Data

Johnson, Angela.
Maniac monkeys on Magnolia Street / by Angela Johnson ; illustrations by John Ward.
p. cm.
Summary: Ten-year-old Charlie adjusts to her move to a new neighborhood
when she befriends Billy, with whom she hunts maniac monkeys, braves
Mr. Pinkbelly's attack cat, and digs for fossils and treasure.
ISBN 0-679-89053-X (trade) — ISBN 0-679-99053-4 (lib. bdg.)
[1. Friendship—Fiction. 2. Moving, Household—Fiction.] I. Ward, John, ill. II. Title.
PZ7.J629Man 1999
[Fic]—dc21 98-33503

Printed in the United States of America
10 9 8 7 6 5 4 3 2 1

For

Truzetta, William, and Charles

(and their wonderful worlds gone by)

CONTENTS

Maniac Monkeys on Magnolia Street

CHAPTER ONE

Maniac Monkeys on Magnolia Street

You can't tell it by the big, peaceful swaying willow trees at the entrance of Magnolia Street, but the neighborhood is full of maniac monkeys.

The first time I saw the willows, I thought of picnics underneath them and maybe even some games of hide-and-seek, too. I never thought of maniac monkeys.

When I first moved to Magnolia Street a few days ago with my brother, Sid, and my mom and dad, I was really missing our old neighborhood on Monroe Street. I missed the chiming of the town hall clock and the smells from the candy factory.

Mostly, though, I missed my friends on Monroe Street.

I didn't see one kid on Magnolia Street the day we moved. Mom and Dad said I'd meet friends soon enough and I should worry more about staying clear of the overpacked rooms so I wouldn't break anything in the boxes.

My brother, Sid, who's twelve, laughed at me and said he didn't think I'd find friends because there weren't any mutants on Magnolia Street. He also said it would be okay if I got in one of the empty boxes and left with the movers.

Funny.

When I whined to Dad and Sid got yelled at, he wasn't so funny then.

He dumped some books out of a box in the living room and crossed his eyes at me. Then he said, "You know, Charlene."

MANIAC MONKEYS ON MAGNOLIA STREET

My name is Charlene, but everybody calls me Charlie 'cause I like it better. Everybody but Sid, that is.

Sid laughed. "I wouldn't get too close to those willows you like so much."

"Why not?" I asked.

"Because those trees are full of maniac monkeys."

"What?" I yelled.

"Maniac monkeys, I said."

I crawled into one of the empty packing boxes and peeked out. I didn't want Sid sending me with the movers.

I said, "Prove it."

Sid got really sad. He came over, sat by my box, and said the cousin of one of his best friends' aunt had told him that maniac monkeys had been stealing kids on Magnolia Street.

"Have you seen any kids since we've been here?" he said.

I knew he was right about that.

"No." But what did he think I was—a baby?

"Don't you wonder where they all are?"

I said, "I just thought they were all grown up and moved away, or they were all away somewhere like summer camp or something."

Sid shook his head and looked at me with that really sad expression again. He patted me on the back and walked away shaking his head. I noticed he'd left the books for me to put away.

I didn't believe Sid, at least not a lot.

But when we'd been on Magnolia Street a few days and I still hadn't seen any kids, I began to wonder if Sid might be right.

I started whining again to Mom and Dad. They said I'd find new friends soon. They said I shouldn't give up hope yet.

Mom and Dad are usually right, and I know that now, 'cause pretty soon I would meet the boy who would be my best friend in the whole world. But I didn't know that yet, though.

One morning, I woke up and he was skating in front of our house. He wore overalls and a baseball cap. He skated up and down the sidewalk.

Hah! Sid was wrong about the monkeys.

For three days, I sat on our front porch and watched the kid skating.

He'd wave to me and I'd wave to him.

On the third day, Sid said, "You'd better go meet him before the monkeys take him away, too."

Later that day, Mom came out on the front porch with cookies and juice. This almost never happened because Mom was usually at work, but she was home for the week because we'd moved.

She called to the skate kid.

"Come on up, boy with the skates who looks

like he might want to eat all these really good store-bought cookies."

I was pretty used to my mom when she said things like that, so I wasn't too embarrassed.

The skating kid rolled to a stop in front of our steps and smiled.

He said, "I'm Billy." Then he ate about half the cookies on the plate before I said, "I'm Charlie."

By the time Mom came back on the porch, the cookies were gone and Billy was telling me all the things I should know about Magnolia Street.

The ice cream truck comes every day around two o'clock, and Mo's Freeze Shack up the street has great ice cream, too.

The fire department opens the hydrants when it's really hot. Everybody stands in the cool water.

The grownups are okay and hand out great candy at Halloween.

Billy said, "Yeah, it's okay around here." I liked Billy 'cause he jumped around when he talked and sometimes even ended up standing on his head.

I decided to ask him about the monkeys, even though I didn't really believe the story. Where would the monkeys come from, anyway?

"Are there really maniac monkeys on Magnolia Street? My brother, Sid, says there are."

Billy said, "I haven't heard about any monkeys."

"Really?"

"Yeah, really. Sounds pretty scary to me, though. Where does your brother say that these monkeys live?"

"He says that they live in the willows."

Billy started laughing so hard he almost rolled off the porch. I started laughing, too. But then I made a decision.

"Let's go looking for them anyway."

The sun was setting on Magnolia Street when me and Billy went looking for the monkeys.

We went to Billy's house to get what he called monkey-catching gear. We took the sofa pillows and a big vase with dragons on it.

Billy asked his mom if it was okay. She was at her computer, which Billy said is always a good time to ask her anything.

Billy's mom said, "Yes, yes, yes."

She didn't put up any fight at all.

He said he once asked if he could paint his bedroom walls with his favorite cartoon heroes. Since she was on her computer, she said, "Do what you want."

But Billy wasn't the best artist. Everything he painted had pointed teeth, was green, and didn't wear clothes.

He had to weed the garden for a whole month.

We dragged the sofa pillows and vase out the door.

"What do we need these things for, Billy?"

"You'll see," he said.

I wanted to know now, but I guessed I could wait. Billy was already a lot of fun to be with. He liked finding things out like I do. Everything was exciting to him. Me too.

So...

We dragged the pillows and the vase along the sidewalk to the willow trees at the beginning of the street.

We sat underneath the beautiful swaying willows with the vase and the pillows beside us and waited.

Billy said, "If a monkey falls out of the tree, he'll fall in the vase. We won't trap him or anything, but we do want to get a look at him. The pillows are to cushion the monkey's fall."

"Pretty good idea," I said to Billy.

We listened to the birds singing. The sounds of Magnolia Street were so wonderful

we just sat quietly as the sun set through the willow branches.

I guess me and Billy finally fell asleep underneath the willow tree, curled up on a cushion, waiting for maniac monkeys.

That man probably shouldn't have shone that flashlight in our eyes like that.

Billy jumped up screaming, "It's the monkeys!"

I grabbed the vase, and the next thing we knew was that the flashlight man had a dragon vase on his head and was pretty mad after he got it off.

He marched us down the street toward Billy's house.

Billy's mom had left her computer by this time.

The streetlights had lit up on Magnolia Street.

My mom and dad must have been taking a

break from unpacking because they were there, too, standing beside Billy's mom.

"Billy, do you think we're in trouble?"

He didn't say anything, though, 'cause everybody—including the man with the flashlight—was looking at us like we had snakes on us.

"Here they are," the flashlight man said.

My mom started coughing. Then Dad came up real close and looked at us.

"Thanks for finding them, Mr. Oliver."

Then he looked at us.

"How did you two get fur all over your faces?"

We both yelled, "The monkeys must have got us!"

That was the last thing I heard from Billy that night because Mom and Dad walked me home. Fast.

As I sat in the tub, I figured that me and Billy were probably just about to be carried off by the maniac monkeys when the flashlight man showed up. We missed all the excitement of the neighborhood looking for us.

I started washing the fur off my forehead and cheeks. Magnolia Street was some great place.

Sid knocked on the door while I was covering my head with bubbles.

He whispered through the door, "I told you about those maniac monkeys. You and that skate kid were almost goners."

Sid went away laughing.

I kept washing off the fur and kept smelling something like cherries and glue.

Weird.

The next morning, I was hanging upside down in our front tree when Billy came over. He climbed up and hung beside me.

"So what's up this morning?"

I started laughing 'cause I figured we probably looked like maniac monkeys swinging upside down from the tree.

"Let's go skating."

I got my bike, and Billy got his skates. After he put his skates on, I pulled him along the sidewalk.

Billy yelled, "What do you think happened to us under the tree? You don't really think the monkeys got us, do you?"

I turned and said, "I've been thinking." But just as I said that, we crashed into the neighbor's shrubs. Mom hollered from the window.

Me and Billy each had to go to our own porches. We'd only known each other for a day and this was the second time we'd been separated. I wasn't alone long 'cause Sid showed up.

"What's up, fur face?"

I said, "I'm on punishment again."

"Too bad," he said.

I didn't believe he was too sad. I was starting

to think that Sid knew more about what had happened last night than he was telling.

I didn't see Billy until a couple of days later.

I was lying under his porch eating an apple when he came out of his house.

I jumped out and scared him. "Where have you been?"

I gave Billy a bite of my apple.

"I've been at my grandma's house. She lives way in the country in the middle of nowhere. Mom said she needed a break. So she left me there for a couple of days. She was pretty happy to see me, though, when she picked me up."

I patted Billy on the back.

"That's what happens to me, too."

Billy asked, "What have you been doing while I've been gone?"

"Mostly sitting on the porch, on punishment."

"Besides that, I mean."

"I've been tracking down monkeys." Then I told Billy the story...

I'd spent the days Billy was gone looking for maniac monkeys. I had gone back to the willow tree and sat underneath it.

All I heard was crickets. I was so comfortable I fell asleep there again. When I woke up, I noticed something was lying beneath me, sticking at my side. Cherry-scented glue stick. *Hmm.*

I ran back to my house and up to my room, and sure enough, what I was looking for was missing. I headed for Sid's room and found something covered up on his chair: one of his old teddy bears, shaved on the belly, and the smell of cherries and glue all around.

Billy looked at me and said, "Sid."

I nodded.

It's going to be a long summer...

I'm already getting used to Magnolia Street,

even though I have a feeling me and Billy might be sitting on our porches, separately, a lot. I still miss the town hall clock chiming and Monroe Street, though.

But who knows...

I think that there may be something always happening on Magnolia Street. I mean, even this morning the maniac monkeys attacked again. Boy, is Sid's bike furry. There must have been about a thousand monkeys.

Oh, well. I guess I'll go with Mom to do a little shopping. Billy is weeding the garden, since he borrowed that vase from his mom to catch the maniac monkeys.

I have to remind Mom that I need more shorts. I'm growing out of the old ones. I need a pair of tennis shoes, too, and oh, yeah, some more glue.

CHAPTER TWO

Charlie P.

I love to jump rope up and down Magnolia Street all day long, and lately that's been all there is to do.

Billy is off at camp for a week and he's already written me three letters. One of them had dirt on it and a picture of Billy standing on his head. I've only known Billy a couple of weeks, but I already miss him.

What else is there to do?

Mom said, "One day, Charlie, you're going to jump rope until your feet fall off." I smiled because she called me Charlie, which I prefer, instead of Charlene.

Billy's real name is Willem, so he says that he

understands how come I hate my name. But his mom only calls him Willem when something gets broken or people show up complaining about him.

How could Mom have known my feet really would fall off?

It's true. Here's the story.

One day, I ran out of the house, picked up my candy cane–striped jump rope, and skipped real slow by Miss Marcia's house. She's an artist who makes statues. She was covered in plaster, sitting on her porch eating muffins.

"Hey, Charlie. What's up?"

I walked into her yard past all the statues she's made. People with baskets on their heads and animals riding bikes crowd each other in Miss Marcia's yard.

I wrapped my jump rope around my waist. "Just jumping and stuff."

Miss Marcia handed me a muffin, and I sat

beside her on the steps while she told me about art and her sculpture. I asked her if she could cover a person with plaster to make a statue.

She said, "It's not something I'd do. I don't think you could get them out of it, and you'd have to be careful about air holes."

I laughed and laughed.

"Is plaster fun to peel off like school glue is when you put it all over your hand?"

Miss Marcia laughed, and some of the plaster fell off by her feet. "No, Charlie, it doesn't come off like glue."

"Too bad. I like peeling glue off my hand. It's like being a snake and shedding my skin or something."

I wiggled around like a snake for a while with my jump rope. Miss Marcia started laughing again, and I finished off the rest of the muffins.

I wiggled out of the yard, then started jumping down the street again. I could still hear Miss Marcia laughing.

Mom says she will laugh at anything. I think she's funny.

The next morning, just as I was about to roll out of bed and start thinking about where I'd jump rope that day, Sid came into my room and hit me with my pillow.

I hate it when he does that.

"Wake up, Spacey."

"Don't do that!" I yelled, loud enough that I hoped Mom or Dad would come up and punish him.

"There's something for you down on the front porch."

"What is it, Sid?"

Sid bonked me in the head with the pillow again and left.

Sometimes I wonder if Sid stays up at night thinking of ways to get on my nerves.

When I finally got up, I ran down the stairs past the kitchen. Everybody was eating, and I knew Mom would make me sit down and have something. I was too fast, though.

I opened the door to the porch and there it was…

A beautiful plaster statue of a girl who looked just like me. She had braids like mine and even a dimple in her chin. Best of all, though, she was jumping rope. Well, not really, because she was a statue and that couldn't be.

I ran over to Miss Marcia's house to thank her.

When I got there, she was in her yard mixing plaster. She pointed to muffins on the porch, but I'd eaten so many the last time that I couldn't face eating even one more.

I said, "I like me in plaster."

Miss Marcia laughed. "Yeah, I like you in plaster, too."

"I guess it was better than my idea of letting you dip me in a big old tub of the stuff from head to toe."

Miss Marcia said, "Yeah, my idea was better."

I hung around long enough to get covered with plaster from head to toe, anyway. Doesn't do to waste a chance of getting stuff all over yourself. When even Miss Marcia said I was covered, it was time to go home.

My statue was beautiful. Dad moved her so she wasn't blocking the door anymore. She stood right by the porch swing.

Everybody who came by our house talked about her.

"Boy, does she look like Charlie," my aunt said when she came to visit.

"Look at that smile on her face," our neighbor Mr. Pinkton said.

"Got that rope in her hand just like Charlie," Mrs. Craig said. I was surprised she was even visiting us from Monroe Street because it was one of my good ideas last summer that made her stop talking to my mom.

Nobody told me that bees wouldn't eat up all the honey that I poured on her porch. I was trying to find their hive. There were always a lot of bees around her house, so I figured they'd come by the millions if I put out honey.

Anyhow, everybody thought Charlie P. (P for "plaster") was great. I'd watch her for hours and hours.

Miss Marcia sure was a good sculptor. I sent her a thank-you note and some flowers I picked...well, some flowers I found.

Everything was going along just fine after Charlie P. came to live on our porch. Even Sid liked her. Sometimes he'd use her as a hat rack, but I got over being mad after I found out she really did look good in hats.

When Billy came home from camp, he was

really impressed. He said it was even better than his leaf art. He'd glued leaves on everything, then everybody. Camp had been okay with Billy.

Those few weeks that Charlie P. stood on the porch were great.

But one day it got so quiet on Magnolia Street that I got bored. Billy was banished to his room, and after you've read a couple of comics, made a snack, tried on your mom's and dad's clothes, then booby-trapped your brother's room—what else is there?

So I got this idea.

It was one of the best ideas I'd ever had, and I have a lot of them. I'd spent most of last summer in the house because of some of my ideas. That's how good they were.

Well, if you can talk your brother (who doesn't know you booby-trapped his room yet) into moving your statue off the porch to the sidewalk, that will take care of the first part.

Sid said, "I don't get why you want this moved."

"I don't know," I said. But I did.

Sid said, "Does Mom know you're moving this?"

I acted as if a horse fly was attacking me and mumbled something Sid couldn't hear as I ran in circles.

Finally, Charlie P. was beside me on the sidewalk.

A bunch of Sid's friends came by and he left with them, but not before they pointed at me and Charlie P. standing next to each other on the sidewalk.

All I'd wanted was to see Charlie P. jump rope beside me. Just once.

I know it sounds funny now, but then...

I mean, she looked so much like me and

everybody was always saying so. And I didn't have a sister, just a brother who teased me and only let me go with him half the time.

Once, Sid told me if you wished for something hard enough, then spun for a minute and jumped up and down twelve times, you'd get your wish.

My wish was that Charlie P. would come to life and jump rope with me.

Well, all that happened was that I found out plaster gets pretty heavy after it dries. And you shouldn't help your wish out by trying to get its leg to bend...

Dad was pulling into the driveway just as Charlie P. fell over (in slow motion) and lost her feet.

Dad came over and stood beside me.

I looked at him and he looked at me, then we both looked at my poor statue. Charlie P. was just lying there with that grin on her face and a jump rope in her hands.

Dad patted me on the head and said, "What's for dinner?" then walked away.

I have such a weird family.

So that's what happened the day my feet fell off.

Dad took Charlie P. to the backyard and dug a hole so she could stand up to her knees. She looks good back there.

Birds land on her, so I hung a feeder off of her. I still visit her, though, when I want to see me.

She's always waiting in the backyard with a big old grin on her face.

One day I'll get Miss Marcia to put her feet back on. Then maybe if I wish hard enough, my jump rope wish for Charlie P. will come true.

Or maybe she'll just hang out forever in the backyard with birds on her head. Which is okay by me, too.

CHAPTER THREE

The Sea

Billy took a crab apple out of his pocket and threw it at the plum tree. A big purple plum fell to the ground. His aim is real good.

"I think I left my favorite baseball cap on the bus, Charlie."

"You're always leaving something on the bus. Remember last week when you left that box of worms on the back seat?"

Billy grinned and ran over to the plum tree and picked up a big purple plum.

"Yeah, I remember. They were pretty dried up by the time I got them back."

For the past two weeks, Billy and I have been

allowed to ride the bus that goes by Magnolia Street. We can only ride it together, though, and you wouldn't believe the things and people we've seen on the bus.

Once, this man walked on dressed as a carrot. He read a book until his stop—a supermarket! There was also the time this woman sang songs about zoo animals really loudly until we got off the bus.

I patted Billy on the back because I know he really loved that baseball cap.

He bit into the plum, and it was so juicy it squirted us both.

Later, right around the time my mom was trying to put two huge pink ribbons in my hair, Billy poked his head through our morning-glory vines.

Billy said, "Mr. George Pinkbelly has my baseball cap."

Mom pulled my hair and looked at Billy.

"Mr. George Pink*ton* you mean, Billy."

Billy smiled at us and pulled a leaf off the morning glories to make a green mustache. Billy's famous on Magnolia Street for giving people nicknames.

"Yeah, I mean Mr. Pinkton."

"How do you know?" I asked, scrunching up so Mom wouldn't pull my whole face off trying to get my braids tight.

"You know him, Charlie. He never wears a hat. Today, though, he is wearing a cap that looks just like mine."

I looked up at Mom. She was shaking her head. I looked at Billy sideways, like he was growing a beard. Everybody knows Mr. Pinkbelly—uh, Pinkton—has a shiny bald head that he is real proud of. He always shows off his head.

Mom finished my hair and kissed me on the side of my face.

"Now you look more like a Charlene than a Charlie."

Billy said I look like a big-haired bunny rabbit.

Then he grabbed my hand, and off we went to get his baseball cap back.

Mr. George Pinkbelly's yard is full of the biggest rosebushes I've ever seen. Everybody always stops outside his gate and looks in. The roses are beautiful.

Mr. Pinkbelly also has an attack cat named Murray. Billy calls him Murray the Mugger because he's been known to sneak up on people from behind and jump them. Murray was sitting in front of the gate.

"Here, Murray," Billy said.

He gave Murray a chunk of ham from his pocket. We opened the gate and ran right past him while he was gobbling up the treat.

Even though Billy thinks Mr. Pinkbelly has his favorite baseball cap, he can't say anything bad about the rose garden. Every color in the rainbow is here.

Standing in Mr. Pinkbelly's yard is like standing in a honey-scented box of crayons.

Me and Billy just stood and breathed.

"Do you think he's wearing my cap in his house, Charlie?"

"Maybe...maybe not."

Billy tiptoed up to the porch and almost fell into a rosebush in a pot. He looked through the screen door.

I said, "Billy, we shouldn't be spying on Mr. Pinkbelly. It's not right."

"Wow!" Billy said.

I moved Billy aside and looked into Mr. Pinkbelly's house.

"Wow!" I said.

Mr. Pinkbelly's house was filled with fish-tanks.

Fishtanks everywhere! On the floor. Built

into walls. Sitting on tables. There were even a few goldfish bowls hanging from the ceiling.

Suddenly Murray was behind us. Boy, can he eat fast. He growled and blocked our way off the porch.

"Good tiger," Billy said.

"Good kitty," I said.

Billy said, "I'll bring you the whole pig next time, okay, Murray?"

But Murray wouldn't move. Now he was hissing. Me and Billy figured there was nowhere left to go but inside.

In a second, we were standing in Mr. Pinkbelly's living room full of fish.

"Hello," someone said.

We looked around the room and all we saw were thousands of fish.

"Hello," we said.

We walked farther into the room and just past a tankful of yellow and blue fish. Mr.

Pinkbelly was busy scooping out tiny fish with a net. He put them in a tiny bowl with some other fish babies so that they could grow up together.

He said, "These fish have just had babies. Have a seat."

Billy and I sat on a soft cushy couch with tropical fish painted all over it. We sank about a mile into it.

Mr. Pinkbelly kept talking as if we'd been invited.

"I love these guppies. When I go to feed them, they do tricks." Mr. Pinkbelly looked at me and Billy real close.

"Fish tricks?" Billy asked.

Mr. Pinkbelly got the joke and laughed. He laughed so hard me and Billy started laughing, too.

Mr. Pinkbelly waved his arms all around.

"Look around, look around," Mr. Pinkbelly said, then went right on tending his fish.

We wandered through the whole house. Sometimes there was furniture, and if there was, it was mostly to hold fish.

Billy pressed his face against one of the tanks. There was magic in his eyes.

Billy was in love with Mr. Pinkbelly's fish. I think he forgot all about his favorite baseball cap. Anyway, Mr. Pinkbelly didn't seem the kind of person who went around taking people's favorite baseball caps off of buses.

We ended up downstairs, where Mr. Pinkbelly was saying as we walked in the room, "Fish are my life."

He offered me and Billy nut-covered brownies and lemonade in tall fish glasses.

Then Mr. Pinkbelly told us about the sea.

He said that when he was young, all he wanted to do was sail away. He became a merchant marine and sailed all over the world. That's how he started loving anything from the sea.

Mr. Pinkbelly told stories about beautiful castles and strange animals. He said that once he thought he might have even seen a mermaid.

Billy's eyes were far away, and maybe he saw it, too.

"Then I got too old to sail anymore, so I came to live on Magnolia Street."

"Don't you miss the sea, Mr. Pinkbe—Pinkton?" I said.

Mr. Pinkton got up off the floor and spun around the room laughing.

"I brought the sea with me!"

We laughed, but it's true. There is a whole sea on Magnolia Street.

"Where did you get Murray?" Billy asked.

"I saved him from the pound," Mr. Pinkton said.

I didn't say it out loud, but I really thought he'd saved the people who worked at the pound from Murray. He'd probably eaten a few people before Mr. Pinkton could get him out of there. I think I'll check the newspaper to see if anybody who works at the pound has been reported missing.

We stayed in Mr. Pinkton's house until the sun started setting. When the sun was coming right through his front window, he opened the blinds.

And then, right here on Magnolia Street, there was magic. The tanks caught the sunlight and glowed...

Mr. Pinkton stood in the center of the room, bowed to us, and said, "The sea."

He sent me and Billy off with a paper bag full of brownies and plastic bags full of guppies.

Murray the Mugger was nowhere to be seen as me and Billy walked out of the house of fish and down the path of roses.

"Great brownies," Billy said while we were sitting on my porch swing holding our fish.

"My mom's going to be surprised by these fish," I said.

"My mom won't be," Billy said.

"I don't know, Billy. Would you say she was surprised by those hundred Japanese beetles you had?"

"Well, she wasn't before they escaped the house I built for them and got into her room."

We swung a while longer until I remembered something.

"Billy, your favorite baseball cap! We didn't get it."

Billy stuffed a whole brownie in his mouth and nodded, then pulled his cap out of his back pocket and smiled a chocolate grin.

"I always did want to see what the inside of Mr. Pinkton's house looked like," he said.

We swung on as the bees buzzed around us and our bag of brownies.

"Me too, Billy," I said.

Then the wind brought the scent of roses through the air, and I'm not sure, but I think it also brought the sea.

CHAPTER FOUR

The Pumpkin Box

It all started because I'm a digger.

Digging is something that I can't help. I have done it since I was a little baby. Dad says I used to try to dig my way out of the playpen.

I don't talk about my digging too much 'cause every time I dig it usually gets me in trouble.

Billy understands about my digging. He says that he knows how hard it can be to break a habit like that. He has a nosy problem and that is pretty hard for him.

When we moved to Magnolia Street, one of the first things I noticed was a vacant lot that looked like the perfect place to dig.

So—

I had been trying not to dig for a long time. But a few nights ago, I dreamed I was in a cave that had treasures and fossils. I woke up digging in my sleep. It was time to do something about this digging problem.

When I asked Billy what I should do about it, he blew a big bubble and spun around on his skates.

"Dig!"

So what was I going to do?

I'd been looking at the empty place across the street from my house for a long time. I decided to drag Billy away from his skating. I had to tell him I was pretty sure that there was a sabertooth tiger or something just waiting for us to dig up.

"Okay, Charlie, where is it?" Billy said, munching on an apple and looking real unhappy.

I expected more from Billy, even though I

know that everybody is not a digger. But I figured that Billy should have been a little happier that I was sharing with him.

"Billy?"

"What?"

"Guess what?"

"What, Charlie?"

"What are you going to do with your part of the sabertooth tiger bones you find?"

"Well, I guess I'll put them together with yours."

"Then you'll help me dig?"

Well, I can say this about Billy, and it's probably why we're friends, if you bug him enough he'll join in sooner or later. He even looked like he might be getting excited about the sabertooth across the street.

While we were both hanging upside down in Miss Marcia's apple tree, Billy asked, "What do we need to dig? You know we have to be careful. We don't want to break any sabertooth bones or anything."

I thought for a while.

"A shovel might be too much. Anyway, my mom won't let me use it after that flower-digging accident I had."

Billy swung by his legs faster.

"What flower-digging accident?"

I closed my eyes, remembering all the dirt and flowers lying around the backyard. I only meant to move the different flowers around so all the colors would be lined up together. Well, I got kind of tired and there was this funny movie on television that Sid was watching.

Mom wasn't happy.

So I just said, "Nothing."

Billy jumped down from the tree.

"My dad has digging tools he uses for the garden out back. They're small, and I'm sure he won't miss them."

"Yeah, he probably won't miss them. I'll get some bags to keep the bones and other stuff we find."

Me and Billy were set.

The digging was hard in the beginning. An old house used to be there, but the only thing left from it was part of the chimney. You wouldn't believe the things we started to find underneath the dirt. I just knew that there had to be a sabertooth or something there.

The first thing we dug up was spoons.

Billy said, "We could clean these things up. They probably are gold!"

Billy put the gold spoons in the bag that was for everything else but bones.

After a while it started getting real hot. I could almost make believe that me and Billy were digging way off in a desert somewhere. We were far away from home with only a little water. We were famous archaeologists.

I would find bones.

Billy would find gold spoons.

I would find fossils.

Billy would find gold spoons.

I would find a whole city buried way down underneath the desert.

And there, Billy would find more gold spoons.

Me and Billy didn't even talk to each other while we dug. We were too busy finding all kinds of treasures.

Billy found a cracked mirror.

I found a scrub brush.

Billy found a bottle with a metal top on it, and I found an old can.

The non-bone bag was filling up, and I noticed that Billy was smiling. Sometimes you just have to bring out the digger in some people.

Just as I was starting to get a little worried 'cause we hadn't run into any bones yet, I hit something with the little hand shovel I had. I took a while to dig it up 'cause I didn't want to wreck any of it.

I'd found something better than a saber-tooth.

It was a pumpkin box.

It was metal and square, and somebody had pasted paper pumpkins all over it.

Billy said, "Can we open it?"

"I don't know."

"Try."

So I did. I just wiggled the lock a little and it opened right up.

And the things inside. I knew then that to be a digger was probably to be one of the most exciting things in the world.

Me and Billy sat side by side and stared at the pumpkin box. Most of the pumpkins had fallen off, but there were a couple left. Inside, there was magic.

Billy looked at me and smiled.

I looked at him and smiled.

The first thing we found in the box was a yo-yo.

It was red and wooden.

We laid it out beside the pumpkin box. We didn't want to put it in the non-bone bag.

Next we found three nickels tied up in a handkerchief. They had buffaloes on them.

After that, we found an old watch. It didn't run.

The only way you could tell we liked everything we found was when we'd say, "Wow." And we said that a lot.

Underneath that, we found a book. It had cowboys on the front of it. The pages were falling apart and we were afraid to open it too much, so we laid it down gently beside the other stuff.

The next thing we found was a note. It was wrapped in wax paper. Billy handed it to me to read, since I was the main digger. The note said:

> *Whoever finds this box must share it. It doesn't matter who you share it with. When you have shared the things in this box, you must put your own treasures in it and bury it again.*
>
> *Signed,*
> *Tracy and David*

The note was brown and falling apart.

And in the bottom of the box was a picture of two kids dressed in funny clothes. The picture was old and a little blurry, but you could still see the kids, and they were smiling.

Billy pointed at the picture, then pointed at my house across the street. Sure enough, there was my tree and house right there in the picture. There is nothing like digging...

We put all the pumpkin box stuff back in the box and loaded up to go home.

Billy thought I should keep the pumpkin box and he should keep the spoons until we figured out what we should do with them.

I slept that night with the pumpkin box right beside my turtle night-light.

I dreamed of Tracy and David. I dreamed that they liked the things that me and Billy liked and did the things that me and Billy did.

Maybe they were diggers, too. One of them must have been, because the box was buried to be dug up. In my dreams, they ran alongside me and Billy. We ate ice cream at Mo's and played and raced around the block for hours. They also got separated a lot and had to go to porch time-out for the whole afternoon.

The next morning, Billy was at my door.

"So who have you been thinking about giving the pumpkin box stuff to?"

I stuffed a doughnut in my mouth and handed Billy one, too. We munched and thought.

It was going to take us a while to think.

We decided to walk around with the box and figure it out. We walked up and down Magnolia Street. We looked at the street like we never had before. Who would we give the pumpkin box treasures to?

I said, "Magnolia Street must have been here a long time. My mom says that the picture in the box is probably sixty years old."

Billy said, "I don't think I know anybody that old. Do I?"

All of a sudden Billy got a big smile on his face, grabbed my hand, and started running toward Mr. Pinkton's. Mr. Pinkton was out in his yard with his roses.

Billy took the watch out of the pumpkin box and handed it to Mr. Pinkton.

"For you," Billy said, and then grabbed me by the hand and ran away. Then he stopped and called to Mr. Pinkton, "So you'll have more time with your fish."

When we got to Billy's yard, I smiled at him.

I dreamed of Tracy and David again that night, and when I woke up the next morning, I knew who we could give the yo-yo to.

The sun was shining real bright out back when Sid sprayed me with the hose. He laughed for a long time.

Mom called from the window, "Sid!"

Sid said, "I didn't do it," like he always does when he's been caught.

I made my mind up then. I went to the pumpkin box and handed the yo-yo to Sid. And the look on his face made me so happy. He was real surprised and said, "Why?"

I said, "'Cause I like you sometimes, and you're a yo-yo, too."

I skipped away to Billy's.

The pumpkin box was great.

When I got to Billy's house, his mom was on the phone.

Billy said, "Mom's calling the library. She says the book in the box is real old and the library may want it."

We smiled at each other.

The next night, Billy said he dreamed of Tracy and David, too.

While Billy skated behind me, I rode my bike to Mo's. I walked up to the counter and handed Mo the nickels. The whole store smelled like cookies and French fries.

Mo looked confused when I said, "For you."

Mo said, "I used to collect these when I was your age."

He wiped his eyes, smiled, and said, "Thanks, kid."

Being a digger must be the best thing you could ever be in this world. You can find things that nobody ever thought could be found again.

Being a digger helps people remember gone things.

Me and Billy have decided to keep the picture of Tracy and David. He will keep it for a week, then I will have it for a week. We will always think about them running and playing on Magnolia Street like us.

We were swinging from the tree in my front yard, wondering what to put back into the pumpkin box.

Billy said, "Why do you think they put what they put in the pumpkin box, Charlie?"

"I don't know. Maybe it was stuff that they found. But it was probably stuff that made them happy."

Billy said, “I figure we can take a little time and think about the stuff that makes us happy before we put it in the pumpkin box.”

And because a serious digger understands these things, I thought Billy was right.

CHAPTER FIVE

The Water Lilies

I could almost smell fall coming as I sat beside Billy on the bus. I think I maybe saw a little gold and red in the trees this morning. That means I've spent almost one whole summer on Magnolia Street. Monroe Street seemed far away.

I know Billy likes to look out the window, so I let him sit on that side. I like sitting in the aisle seat because then you can watch everybody who gets on and off the bus.

Me and Billy decided to sing the duck song.

It's real easy to learn, and for some reason it sounds best when you're on a bus or in a small room with a lot of people around.

I started the song just about the time the bus driver drove over the Magnolia Street Bridge.

It goes…

Duck, duck, duck, duck,
Quack a lot of ducks.
Duck, duck, duck, duck,
Drive a yellow truck.

Billy says that the more you sing it, the funnier it gets.

He says it really gets funny in the car when your parents start covering their ears and finally say that they will pull the car over if you don't stop that racket.

So we sang till we almost lost our voices.

I think that me and Billy have nice voices. When we hit high notes, our voices crack and we really sound like ducks. We should think about starting a band or something.

Duck, duck, duck, duck,
Quack a lot of ducks.
Duck, duck, duck, duck,
Drive a yellow truck.

We sang about ten choruses.

Billy said, "That was pretty good."

"Yeah. I think everybody enjoyed it. Especially those people who keep looking at us."

A woman with a shopping bag, a man with a tennis racket, and this couple carrying a big picture frame stared at us the whole time.

Billy pressed his lips against the window.

He said, "We should have asked them to join in."

I swung my legs out in front of me and wondered when they'd be long enough to touch the floor of the bus.

I said, "You think they would have joined in?"

Billy looked around, and the woman with the bag frowned at him. I think she thought that he was going to sing again.

"No."

"Charlie, I wish it was colder. I could make wet lips all over the bus window."

I guess you can't have everything you want. We just had to be happy that while we were on the bus we were good at singing the duck song.

We rode to the art museum with the statues outside the doors.

Me and Billy love the art museum.

It's one of the places we get to go to alone on the bus because we don't have to make transfers or wait at bus stops.

The bus dropped us off right in front of the museum. There weren't many cars in the parking lot, so I knew we'd have most of the museum to ourselves.

Billy looked at me and I looked at him.

"Yes!"

This is what the museum is like when you first walk in it.

Cool and sort of shadowy.

You know that you're someplace that is different and wonderful. We come here as much as we can.

Billy and me walked hand in hand through the lobby. We stopped to read what was showing at the museum that week and what would be showing in a few weeks.

I said, "Why do we even look at what is showing? We always go to the same place every time."

"Yeah, we do."

"We should look at more things in the museum, Billy."

"Yeah, you're right. There's a whole lot we haven't seen."

We walked by a group of Girl Scouts who were being shown around by a guide.

Me and Billy headed to our spot. To get there, we had to go by the room that has all the armor and old weapons. Then we had to go by the room with all the headless statues. I like this room, but haven't stayed there much.

After that, we walked down a lighted hall that has pictures of lots of old men with beards.

Billy likes this hallway. He always stops and poses in front of some of the paintings. Today was the same as always.

"How do I look?" Billy said.

He was standing with his hand in the air and frowning like a bearded man in the painting. The man was sitting on a horse and staring straight ahead.

"Cool," I said. "But why do you think the man is frowning so much?"

"Scratchy underwear," Billy said.

We stayed in the hall for a little time making faces at all the men in the paintings.

I said, “They need to laugh a little.”

So we laughed for them.

We marched down the hall laughing as hard as we could, until we got to the door that led to our spot.

Our spot is a secret place.

We’re starting to think that nobody else in the world knows about it. There’s ivy that grows up the brick walls that surround the garden. There are wooden benches that sit beside the walls. But the best part of the garden is the lily pond right in the middle of it all.

It’s so quiet here.

You forget where you are, and you really forget that you’re in a museum full of pictures of frowning old men.

Billy sat on one bench, and I sat on the bench on the opposite wall.

I whispered to Billy, “Wouldn’t it be nice to be a frog here? We could just hang around the pond and eat flies and sit on the lily pads all day long..."

"And when we wanted something to do, we could hop through the museum," he said.

"We could go in the room that has the huge picture of the water lilies. We could sit there all day and not move," I said.

"We'd have to be careful."

"Yeah, somebody might sit on us or something," I agreed.

"Frogs might only be welcomed out here in the garden."

"Too bad," I said.

We sat in the garden for a long time and listened to the water and the quiet.

When me and Billy were done sitting in the garden, we walked back through the door and down the hall past the frowning old men.

Usually we head for the bus, but today we decided to go sit in the room with the huge painting of the water lilies. We sat on the bench in front of the lilies, and I could almost hear the water.

I looked at Billy and said, "Ribbit."

I love going to the museum.

When we got back on the bus, we had the same driver, who shook his head at us as we showed him our bus passes.

He said, "Are you two going to sing that duck song again?"

I said, "Did you like it?"

He said, "No."

Billy giggled. "Then we'll sing something else."

And we did.

Ribbit, ribbit, ribbit,
Croaking like a frog.
Ribbit, ribbit, ribbit,
Eating flies on a log.

Oh, yeah, me and Billy should really start a band.

We sang the frog song through the city and all the way over the Magnolia Street Bridge and back home again, where the trees, I saw, really were turning red and gold.

CHAPTER SIX

The Story That Twists Around

I snuggled down under my hummingbird blanket and thought how some days are so much fun you wish that they wouldn't end.

Today was one of those days. I'd had fun, but I was tired at the end because the day had gotten twisty.

Mom came to my door. She stood there and whispered, "You asleep, Charlie?"

I said, "Yes, I'm asleep."

She laughed and walked over to my bed and turned on my turtle night-light.

She said, "Scoot over."

I did, and she lay beside me and started looking around my room. She pointed at my collection of leaves in the corner.

I love leaves and pick them up any time I can. I tape them to my walls and the floor. That corner of my room looks like the woods. Billy says all I need in my room is a creek, then I'd really be in the woods.

Mom looked at me and asked, "Are you sad?"

When I didn't say anything, she kept asking me questions.

"Are you mad?"

"Did you have a good day?"

"Do you want to yell? Where have you been all day?"

I finally grabbed my head 'cause it felt like what the tennis ball that Sid bounces against the house must feel like.

I told Mom, "I really want a snack. Maybe a whole lot of crackers and sweet pickles."

Mom smiled 'cause she knew that's my

favorite thing to eat and I must be okay if I wanted to eat it.

"I'll be back in a minute," she said.

When she came back, I took the plate from her and munched everything up in a couple of minutes.

"Wow," Mom said. "You ate that up like you were a vacuum cleaner."

That made me laugh. She grabbed me by the hand and pulled me out of bed. We walked down the stairs out to the porch. I was in my pajamas. Me and Mom sat on the porch and watched fireflies. We swung for a while, then stopped and just listened to the crickets.

Mom said, "So what about your day, Charlie-poo?"

"Mom!" I don't like it when she calls me Charlie-poo.

"It was a crazy day."

"Well, tell me about it, Charlie."

I said, "Okay, but it's a story that twists around."

Mom tucked her feet beneath her and tickled my neck.

"That's okay. I've got time for a twisty story."

The fireflies lit up the front yard just as I began.

So—the twisty story.

"Billy wasn't home when I went around to the side door of his house this morning and knocked for about five minutes. He usually is hanging around there 'cause he keeps his earthworms and things on a built-in shelf right by the door."

"The doors were open, so I figured Billy and his mom had run out to the store for a few minutes. I decided to sit in the tire swing in his backyard and wait for them to get back...

"Mom, can I have a tire swing put up in the front yard tree? I know if I swing high enough and fast enough, I can touch the tops of passing cars."

"No, you can't have a tree swing, Charlie. What about the story?"

"I told you it was a twisty story."

"Oh."

"Well, I waited in Billy's backyard most of the morning."

Mom said, "Most of the morning, Charlie?"

"Well, it felt like most of the morning. I had time enough to build a house for the ants in Billy's backyard and move some of his dad's flowerpots the way I like them."

"Charlie, you shouldn't touch other people's things."

"I didn't touch that much, I just decorated Billy's backyard. But the funny thing happened just as I was about to leave. This big van pulled into Billy's driveway and a bunch of people poured out."

"Who were they?" Mom asked.

"That's not important right now. What is important is that they had a lot of kids and they looked like they might be fun. Everybody was laughing and piling out of the van.

"Before I could say anything, this man with a big cowboy hat came over and asked me, 'Where are they?'

"Well, I told him that I thought they had just run out for a minute. He laughed real loud while other people dragged out coolers and all kinds of food. These two teenagers even brought out a badminton set from the van."

"Wow, Charlie. Looks like Billy's family was going to have a picnic," Mom said.

"Yep, it sure did look like that. Billy hadn't told me anything about it. I knew I was going to have fun, though, 'cause everybody was so friendly."

"What were some of the kids' names?"

"There was Keisha, Raymond, Max, Ahmed, and Cinder. Mom, can I change my name to Star Bright? I don't think I'm a Charlene."

"We've talked about this before, Charlie. Tell me more about Billy's family and the picnic."

"Well, I told everybody to go in and make themselves at home. So all the adults went on in after they had set up all the picnic stuff in the backyard. Somebody accidentally squashed my ant house."

"I'm sorry about that," Mom said.

"That's okay. I can build another one. Anyway, the kids were all about my age, so they stayed outside with me. I told them that there were some okay things to see on Magnolia Street."

"So what did you all do?"

"Well, I was going to wait for Billy, but I think the kids had been in the van too long. They wanted to take a long walk around the neighborhood."

"So where did you take them?"

"I took them everywhere, Mom. I took them to the ravine and we threw rocks down into it. I took them to the back of the pudding factory. We stood there forever, smelling everything."

"They enjoyed that, huh?"

"Yeah, Cinder enjoyed it so much she asked if we could get pudding if we knocked on the door."

"Did you all knock?" Mom asked.

"No, her brother Raymond told her not to be greedy, so we forgot about it. Then we went over to the park and hung around on the playground and stuff. Keisha and Raymond had skateboards."

"Did you guys have fun?"

"Yeah, we did. I liked all the kids a lot. After we were done in the park, we went to Mo's for tacos and ice cream. Everybody said they had room for more food, too. And that was great 'cause their parents brought a ton."

"So that's what you did all afternoon."

"We stayed away for a long time. We left Billy's house a couple of hours before lunch and didn't come back till I saw Dad pulling into our drive."

"Well, that was about three-thirty this afternoon."

"When we came back, though, the grownups were barbecuing out back and playing badminton and sitting around the picnic table talking and laughing and dancing."

"Were Billy and his mom and dad there yet?"

"Nope."

"So what did you do, Charlie?"

"I played badminton and ate a hamburger and danced like everybody else did. I had a good time. I came home a little before you called me in for dinner."

"Well, I'm glad Billy's relatives were nice, but I still don't understand the twisty part of this story."

"The twisty part of the story happened when all the relatives were loading up to leave and Billy and his mom and dad pulled into the driveway."

"Well, where had they been? Don't tell me that they had gone to the relatives' house by mistake."

"Nope, they'd gone to the state fair for the day. I only remembered that then."

"That's too bad that they'd missed the picnic and the relatives."

"Yep, I thought so, too."

"You usually have a pretty good memory, Charlie."

"Yeah, usually."

"I'm sorry that Billy's family reunion didn't work out."

"Me too. Billy loves picnics."

"Maybe they'll plan another get-together."

"Maybe they will, even though none of the

people were related to Billy's family. It turned out that the people had come to the wrong street and the wrong house. Their relatives live on Magnolia *Drive*. They'd never been there before."

Mom started laughing so loud I thought she would scare all the fireflies.

"So, Charlie, *that* was the twist?"

"Pretty twisty, huh?"

"You had some day."

"Oh, yeah, it was pretty okay. I'm tired now."

"I'll bet you are, entertaining Billy's not relatives like that. Time to go up to bed now."

"Okay, but Mom. Can I have a tree swing?"

Mom pulled me toward the door.

"Time for bed, Charlie-poo."

"Mom!"

CHAPTER SEVEN

Us and the Wind

When the wind blows on Magnolia Street, it can bring just about anything or anyone blowing by.

It's been a fun summer, and even though I'll soon be going to a new school, Billy says I'll like it.

Today we climbed up into the tree in front of my house. We swayed there, enjoying the windy day. All kinds of things flew by us.

We both sat wide-eyed and said, "Wow."

This is what we saw:

Clothes from people's lines.

A baby stroller full of vegetables.

Garbage can lids and people chasing them.

There was even a big old bowl of popcorn that Miss Marcia had been spray-painting. The purple and red popcorn looked so pretty flying around the neighborhood. We watched it all from our perch in the tree.

Me and Billy started to imagine that we were in the sails of a tall ship. All the things blowing by us on Magnolia Street became big waves of water.

When anyone walked by our sailboat, we called out, "Ahoy!"

Then they just looked all over the place trying to find out where the voices came from. Nobody ever looked up, though. Me and Billy sailed along. We passed islands and dolphins who swam along beside us as we went farther out into the ocean.

Billy yelled, "Sea monster!" when Mrs. Bateman went running by in the funniest-

looking hat I've ever seen. She really did look like a monster in that hat. We were rescued from the monster when her hat blew off and she chased it down the street—I mean, ocean.

Billy said, "I love sailing," and I knew what he meant as we floated on past Magnolia Street.

When me and Billy were just about to discover a new island, we were brought back to Magnolia Street, the wind, and the tree. We looked down and there he was.

A boy in overalls and a straw hat heard us calling, "Ahoy!"

Squinting into the wind, he looked up at us and yelled, "Who's up there? What are you two doing? Can I climb up, too? How long have you been up in the tree?"

The boy kept asking questions and jumping like a frog every time we answered one. When he ran out of questions, he spun in circles, then flew like an airplane around the tree.

He looked as if he belonged in the wind as he flew around our imaginary sailboat.

I asked, "What's your name, kid?"

The boy stopped flying and jumped straight up and grabbed on to one of the lower branches, then started swinging.

"My name's Lump."

Lump kept swinging.

Billy said, "Where do you live?"

Lump let one hand go and pointed to somewhere down the street.

I said, "Lump from down the street, huh?"

Lump said, "I live around. One minute I was on my street, the next I'm here."

Billy said, "I think I saw you in school last spring."

Well, on most days Billy pretty much thinks the way I do about certain things. I mean, there have been a few times when we didn't see things alike. Most of the time, though...

So when I said, "Lump from down the street," I think that Lump's name suddenly struck Billy as real funny, because it was only a few seconds later that Billy fell out of the tree laughing.

I worried that Billy might have hurt Lump's feelings, and that isn't like Billy.

But when I looked down through the branches, Billy was sitting on the grass beside Lump and they were talking about dolphins and whales.

I jumped down and sat beside Lump.

I said, "What's up?"

Lump pointed to the wind and all the things blowing by in it. I started to smile. Billy had a big old grin on his face, too. I think Lump is one of those people who make you smile all the time. I have an uncle like that. At family picnics, everybody circles around him and always leaves smiling.

Lump told us that he hasn't lived in the neighborhood long. He came to live with his aunt and uncle. His uncle makes pudding and gets paid for it.

I said, "I didn't think anybody could be that lucky. They should save those jobs for kids. I don't think grown people can really appreciate a job like that."

Billy agreed and nodded his head.

Lump said, "I think my uncle likes it. He's gained a whole lot of weight since he started working there. My aunt keeps trying to get him to start running or something, but he says he'll only run when he's being chased."

Me and Billy looked at each other and smiled.

We liked Lump.

Soon he was telling us about where he used to live and how it wasn't as windy as it is here on Magnolia Street. He said he never met anybody sailing a boat up in a tree there, either. He was glad that Billy fell out of the tree, though, and did we know where he could get some really good ice cream?

Just as me and Billy were about to tell him about Mo's Freeze Shack, our heads were covered in blowing newspapers that must have escaped from somebody's recycling bin.

We took the newspapers off our heads and lay back on the grass laughing and listening to the wind howl and watching the clouds rush by until Sid came by on his bike and said, "You all waiting for somebody to drop something on you?"

Lump looked at me.

I said, "Don't pay any attention to that creature on the bike. He's just this kid who climbs in our house through a window now and then and eats up all our food. My parents feel sorry for him, so they let him stay. We figure he'll go away on his own after a while and catch up with his real family. He says he's related to us, but I think that's just to get birthday presents and things."

Sid crossed his eyes, parked his bike, and went into the house.

I smiled at Billy and Lump.

A windy day just blows in all kinds of things to do.

Soon me, Billy, and Lump were chasing run-away belongings from all the neighbors down the sidewalks and into all the yards.

Billy decided that it would be fun to wear everything we found. Lump grabbed the first thing that blew by him.

In a few minutes, I was wearing a straw hat with fruit and a horn on top of it and Billy was wearing an apron that said KISS THE COOK.

The strangest outfit of all, though, was Lump's. He was wrapped in a baby blanket and had a green plastic bucket on top of his head.

KISS
THE
COOK

We marched down Magnolia Street. It was just us and the wind.

Miss Marcia waved to us and called, "Got time to visit?"

We ran up her sidewalk and sat on the steps. She was covered in yellow paint.

I said, "This is our new friend, Lump."

Miss Marcia stopped painting a big piece of plywood.

"Nice to meet you, Lump. Windy, isn't it?" Then she pointed to the marshmallow brownies on the table and talked about trains and her flower garden and how she hoped the wind wouldn't blow it away.

When we'd eaten most of the brownies, we thanked Miss Marcia and marched back down the walk.

Lump said, "I like her. She didn't even ask me my real name like most grownups do. She didn't say anything about our clothes, either."

Billy said, "Yeah, she's okay. She's not nosy, and she thinks 'most anything we do is funny."

Lump smiled back at Miss Marcia, who was painting up a storm. He started running down the sidewalk, blanket blowing. Billy and I took off after him.

The wind began to get stronger. We ran up and down the street a few times, but ended up in front of my house.

We lay down in front of the tree and listened to the wind again.

Suddenly Lump stood up.

He said, "If you want to go somewhere you've always wanted to go, all you have to do is spin around three times, put your arms out like you're flying, close your eyes, and there you'll be."

So me, Billy, and Lump sailed on past the ocean.

But the whole time, if we looked out the

corner of our eyes, we could spot the willows that welcome you to Magnolia Street and Miss Marcia's house and Mr. Pinkton's roses. Once, I could even see Sid's bike as a dolphin racing past us in our sailboat. A few times me, Billy, and Lump even caught sight of the tree branches we sailed away in.

Mom came out and snapped an instant picture of us in the tree.

We sailed until the sun started to go down and we all got called in to eat.

We ran up and down the street returning the windy day stuff back to where we thought it belonged, then we said good night to each other and went home.

It came to me now just as I was about to fall asleep that Lump had been looking for us when we first met him. Now he was here with me and Billy, and it's like we've been together forever.

I looked at the picture of us all in the tree. I think it may be a good idea to put the picture Mom took of us into the pumpkin box. Maybe we'll find more things for it later.

I hope I have nice dreams of Billy, Lump, and me on Magnolia Street and hope the wind always brings us wonderful things.

Angela Johnson is the author of many books for young readers, including *Do Like Kyla*, illustrated by James Ransome, *Toning the Sweep*, for which she received the Coretta Scott King Award, and *Songs of Faith*. Born in Tuskegee, Alabama, she moved with her family to Ohio at a young age. Although she has lived there ever since, she enjoys traveling—when she isn't busy writing or wrangling gigantic goldfish. She is currently at work on another book about Charlie and her adventures on Magnolia Street.